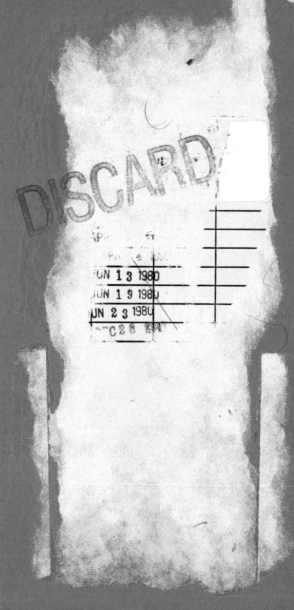

That's Enough for One Day, J.P.!

That's Enough for One Day, J.P.!

by SUSAN PEARSON
Pictures by KAY CHORAO

The Dial Press, New York

Library of Congress Cataloging in Publication Data
Pearson, Susan.
That's enough for one day, J. P.
Summary: J. P. prefers staying indoors but his mother
insists he go out to play, only to regret it later.
[1. Mothers and sons—Fiction] I. Chorao, Kay. II. Title.
PZ7.P323316Th   [E]   76-42923
ISBN 0-8037-8566-6
ISBN 0-8037-8567-4 lib. bdg.

For Nippy

John Philip Jamison liked to read.

On Thursday he read a book about ladybugs. His mother said, "You need some fresh air."

On Friday he read about dragonflies. His mother said, "You need some exercise."

On Saturday he read about spiders. His mother said, "John Philip, you'll make yourself sick with your nose in a book all the time. Get outside and play this instant."

John Philip felt fine. But he put on his jacket and his base-ball cap, tucked his book under his arm, and went down-stairs.

"Have a good time," his mother said at the back door as she took the book away from him.

"This is silly," said John Philip.

"Hey, J.P. Over here!" Seth and the gang were playing baseball in the vacant lot behind John Philip's house. "You can be on my team," said Seth.

John Philip stepped up to bat.

Crack went the bat against the ball. *Smash* went the garage window.

Mother came to the back door. "What's going on?"

"I hit a home run," said John Philip.

"Well, hit a home run somewhere else," said Mother.

"Let's play in the treehouse instead," said Seth.

The gang climbed the rope ladder and pulled it up after them.

"Let me up too," shouted Sandy.

"Scram," said John Philip.

"I'll tell Mama," screamed Sandy.

"Go ahead," said John Philip.

"What's going on?" Mother called from the back steps.

"This treehouse is for men," said John Philip. "Not for baby brothers."

"That treehouse is for everybody," said Mother. "You let your brother up this instant."

"I've gotta go home," said Seth.

John Philip went next door. Old Lady Hartzog was painting her house.

"Can I help?" said John Philip.

"Sure, J.P.," said Old Lady Hartzog. "Just grab yourself a brush."

John Philip painted for half an hour. Then Old Man Hartzog came outside with his garden shears. "What on earth's the matter with you, Emily," he said. "That child is spilling paint all over my rosebushes."

John Philip's mother leaned out a window. "What's going on?" she called across the yard.

"I've been fired," said John Philip.

"Leave Mrs. Hartzog alone," said Mother.

"Sorry, J.P.," said Old Lady Hartzog.

John Philip sat on his own front steps. He put his elbows on his knees and his chin in his hands.

Nancy was playing with her dog Scott. "Hey, Nancy," John Philip shouted. "You wanna go fishing?"

"Sure, J.P.," Nancy shouted back. "But we gotta dig some worms first."

119226

John Philip got an old can from the garage, and they began to dig. Scott dug too.

"Hey, look at this one," said Nancy.

"It's a beauty all right," said John Philip.

"So was my garden until you two got into it. I just planted those bulbs last week, John Philip," said Mother. "Go dig somewhere else."

"I wish *she'd* go somewhere else," said John Philip very quietly so only Nancy could hear.

Sally was washing her car across the street. John Philip and Nancy walked over to watch. "Want some help?" said John Philip.

"Okay," said Sally. "You soap it up, and I'll hose it down."

John Philip and Nancy soaped one side of the car and Sally followed behind them with the hose. "Hey, J.P.," said Sally. John Philip turned around. Sally aimed the hose right at him. Then she squirted Nancy too.

"John Philip," called Mother. "Time for lunch."

"C'mon back later," said Sally. "You can help wax."

John Philip went across the street and into his house. "What's for lunch?" he said.

Mother turned around and looked at him. "You are a filthy mess!" she said. "Take those clothes off and go to your room. And STAY there. You've had enough fresh air for one day, and I've had enough of you!"

John Philip went upstairs. He put on dry clothes. Then he stretched out on the floor on his stomach and opened his book about spiders.

Susan Pearson

was born in Boston and grew up in Massachusetts, Virginia, and Minnesota. She now lives in New York City, where she is a children's book editor. Ms. Pearson is also the author of *Monnie Hates Lydia* and *Izzie,* which was a *New York Times* Outstanding Book of the Year and a Child Study Association Book of the Year in 1975.

Kay Chorao

was born in Indiana and grew up in Cleveland, Ohio. She studied art at the Chelsea School of Art in London and the School of Visual Arts in New York City, where she now lives with her husband and three children. Ms. Chorao is the author/artist of *Molly's Moe,* a Junior Literary Guild Selection, and has illustrated numerous children's books, including *Albert's Toothache,* a 1975 ALA Notable Book.